THE magic ROCKET

by Steven Kroll
illustrated by Will Hillenbrand

Holiday House/New York

For Kendall and Phyllis Merriam
S.K.

For Johnathan
W. H.

Text copyright © 1992 by Steven Kroll
Illustrations copyright © 1992 by Will Hillenbrand
All rights reserved
Printed in the United States of America
First Edition
Library of Congress Cataloging-in-Publication Data
Kroll, Steven.
The magic rocket / by Steven Kroll : illustrated by Will
Hillenbrand.—1st ed.
p.   cm.
Summary: Felix's dog, Atom, is abducted by a flying saucer
and Felix must rescue him by following in a magic rocket.
ISBN 0-8234-0916-3
[1. Unidentified flying objects—Fiction.   2. Imagination—
Fiction.]   I. Hillenbrand, Will, ill.   II. Title.
PZ7.K9225Mag   1992   91-10114   CIP   AC
[E]—dc20

FELIX LOVED ROCKETS. He had big rockets and little rockets. He had plastic rockets and metal rockets. He had noisy rockets and silent rockets.

Every day, Felix and his dog Atom went to a big
store called Space Toys. For weeks Felix had been
admiring the rocket in the window.

It was different from other rockets. It was long and
thin and gold. It had three booster rocket engines and
a shiny cockpit. Whenever Felix looked at it, it seemed
to glow mysteriously.

On Felix's birthday, his dad came home with a big box tied up in ribbon.

"Happy birthday, Felix," said Dad.

Felix tore away all the paper. He reached inside and pulled out the gold rocket.

"Oh, wow!" he said. "It's just what I wanted."

That night, after finishing his ice cream and birthday cake, Felix went upstairs to his room and put on his pajamas. He played with his new rocket for a long, long time. Then he climbed into bed and went to sleep.

A few hours later, a beeping noise woke Felix. He sat
up in bed. The noise was coming from outside.

Felix rushed to the window. A silvery-red flying saucer
was landing in the backyard next to Atom's doghouse!

The beeping noise stopped. A weird-looking creature
climbed to the ground. Atom rushed out of his doghouse,
barking and snarling.

Felix rubbed his eyes. Was he dreaming, or was he really seeing a creature from Outer Space? As he was wondering what to do, the creature grabbed Atom, climbed back into the flying saucer, and took off.

"Atom!" cried Felix. Just then, a humming noise began to fill the room.

It was coming from the new rocket. The rocket began to glow. It glowed brighter and brighter, and as it glowed, it began to grow.

Quickly Felix took it off the shelf, but in his hands, it kept on growing. Soon it was longer than his arm.

"I'd better take this outside," Felix said. He hurried into some clothes. By the time he got the rocket downstairs and into the backyard, it was almost as tall as he was.

He stood it on end in the grass. In a few minutes, it was higher than the house!

Suddenly the humming noise stopped. The rocket stopped growing, the cockpit's bubble top sprang open, and a golden ladder unfolded all the way to the ground.

A voice came from inside. "You must climb up to the cockpit. Don't worry. You will be safe."

The rocket flashed on and off as Felix grabbed a rung of the ladder and began to climb.

When he stepped into the cockpit, he saw a computer with an enormous screen.

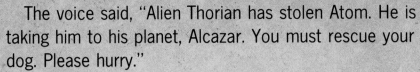

The voice said, "Alien Thorian has stolen Atom. He is taking him to his planet, Alcazar. You must rescue your dog. Please hurry."

The voice was coming from the computer.

"Wow!" said Felix. "I'm going to save Atom!"

He slid into the captain's seat. He closed the cockpit and pressed a button on the computer that said "Power." The rocket's three booster engines fired. With a great *whoosh,* he was off!

Captain Felix guided his craft higher, and a map of the sky appeared on the screen. It showed Felix zooming closer to the flying saucer.

A small light blinked on the computer. A message flashed on the screen: "Line up rocket to face dog in saucer. Push red button on right. Splatterizer ray will zap dog back to rocket."

As Felix was about to get into position and push the red button, the saucer swerved around. It started heading toward him!

On the screen, Felix could see Thorian getting ready to shoot him with a laser gun.

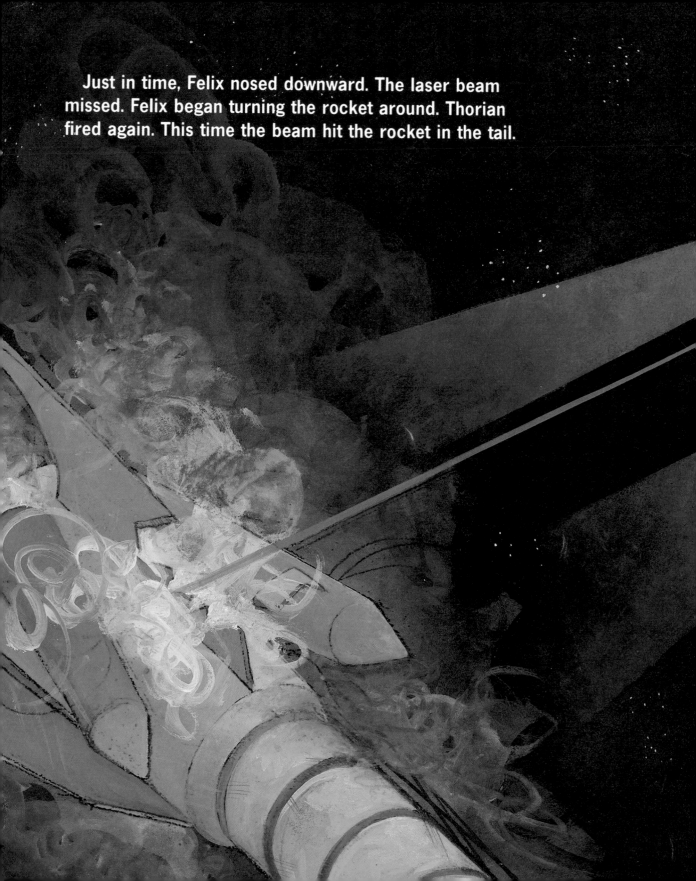

Just in time, Felix nosed downward. The laser beam missed. Felix began turning the rocket around. Thorian fired again. This time the beam hit the rocket in the tail.

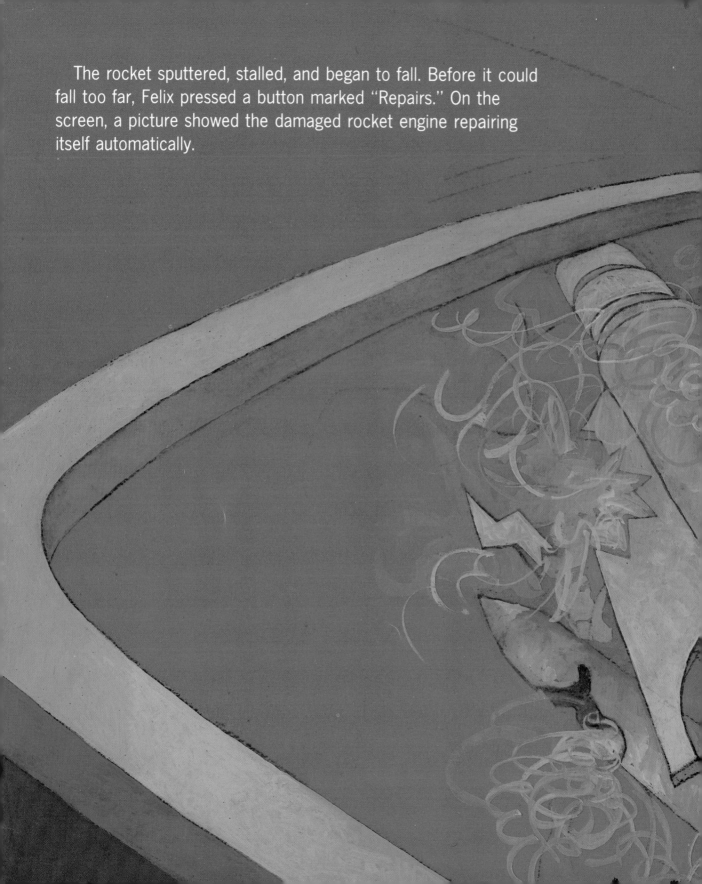

The rocket sputtered, stalled, and began to fall. Before it could fall too far, Felix pressed a button marked "Repairs." On the screen, a picture showed the damaged rocket engine repairing itself automatically.

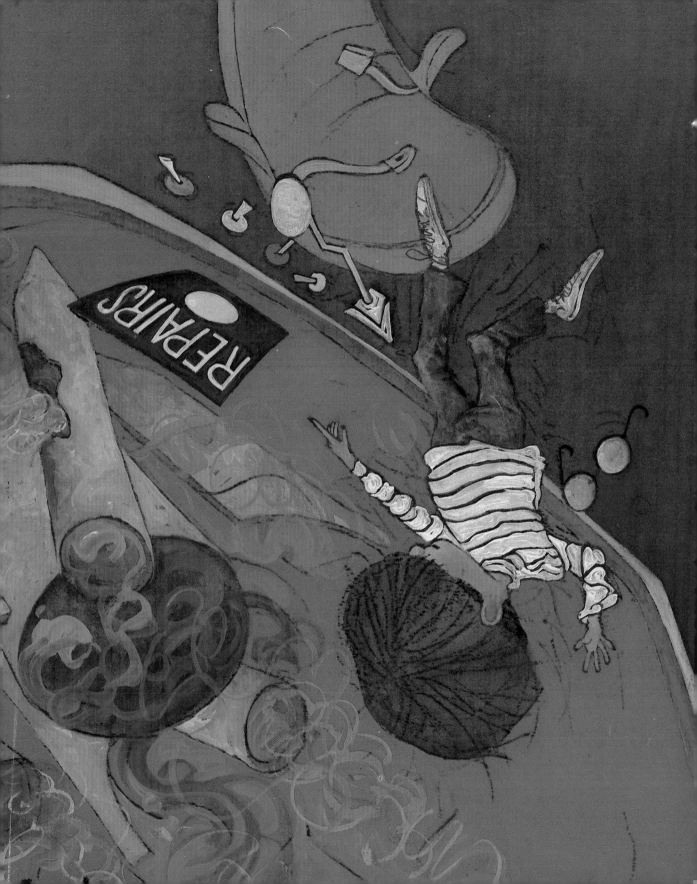

By now the flying saucer was far ahead. Felix flipped a switch marked "Extra power." The rocket shuddered and lurched forward.

In seconds, Felix caught up with Thorian. This time, he was able to line himself up with the saucer and push the red button.

Suddenly, Atom appeared in his lap!

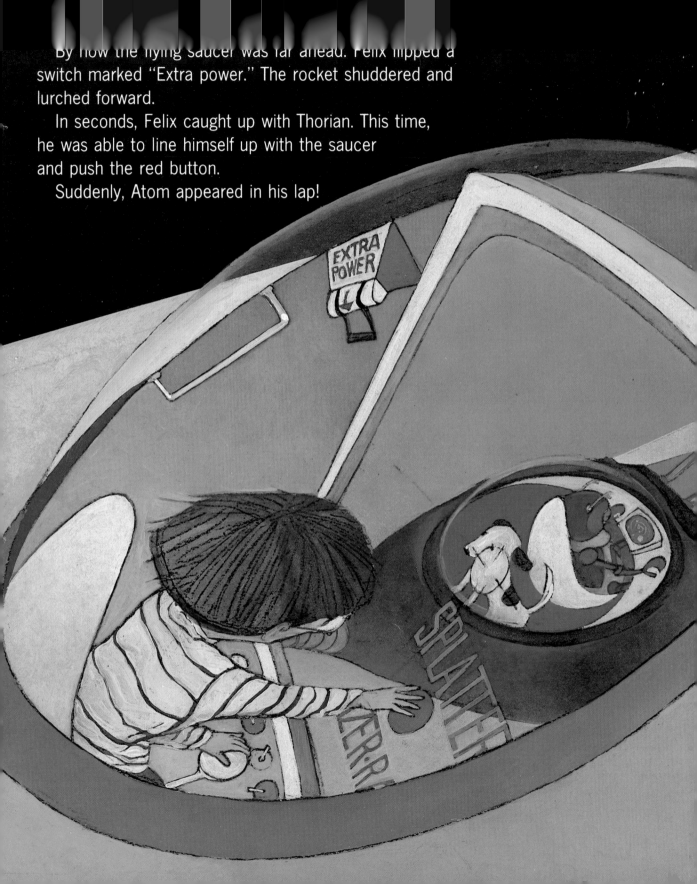

Felix couldn't believe it. "Atom, it's you," he said. He hugged him, and Atom licked his face all over.

The light was blinking on the computer again. Another message flashed on the screen: "Push green button. Zap Thorian back to Alcazar."

Felix pressed the green button. There was a flash, and the flying saucer disappeared to Alcazar.

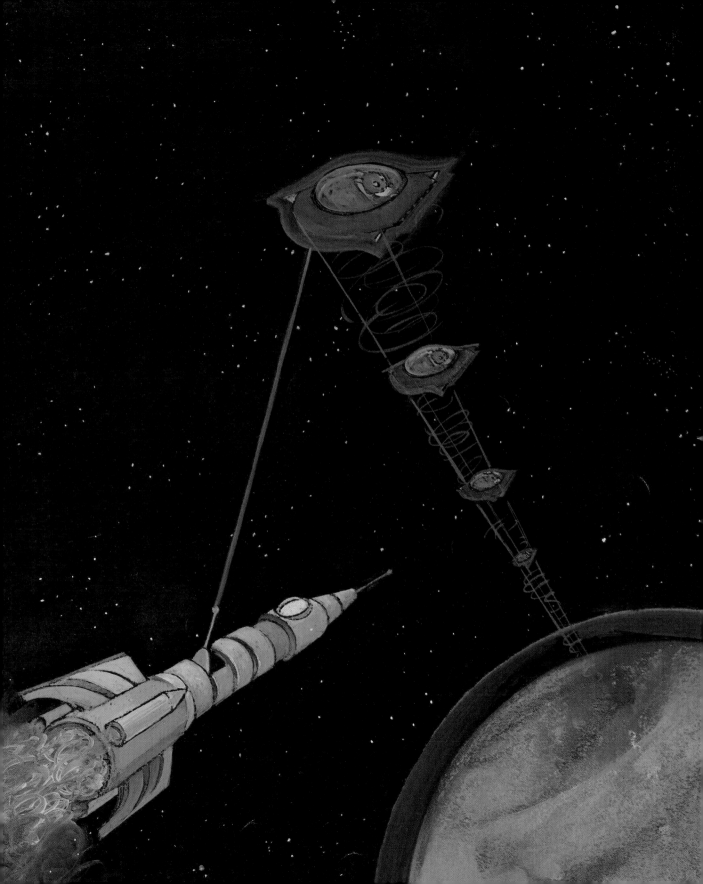

"Congratulations," said the computer voice. "Now it's time to go home."

Felix patted Atom on the head and started back to Earth. The rocket passed Saturn, Jupiter, and Mars. When Felix looked out of the cockpit, he saw his backyard. There was a circle of light in the grass.

Felix pressed the button marked "Land."
The rocket glided down into the circle. When
Felix and Atom climbed down the ladder, the
rocket shrank back to its original size.

Felix carried the rocket upstairs and
returned it to the shelf.

He shook his head and sighed.
"You are some rocket," he said.

Then he climbed into bed and let Atom curl up
beside him. As he was about to drift off to sleep, the
rocket flashed on and off one last time.

"Good night, rocket," said Felix.
"Good night, Felix," said the voice of the computer.
Felix smiled, put his arm around Atom, and went
back to sleep.